AMIR BECKFORD KURTIS YATES SARAH RAMOS-RIVERA JAN VARGAS AZIYAH JAWARA VALERIE HERNANDEZ

WE MATTER:
SIX STUDENTS & THEIR PROTEST

ILLUSTRATED BY CAMERON WILSON

Dear FLOC Family,

2020 was a year like no other, for a myriad of reasons. At FLOC, we gave our students an opportunity to talk about how they felt about the things they were seeing and experiencing, and from those conversations, we knew we needed to find a way for our students to express themselves and of course, learn a new skill along the way. From those conversations came their book, "We Matter: Six Students and Their Protest." These stories are from the perspective of each of our students. These are their feelings, their dreams, and their words. I am so proud of this group of students and am even more excited to share their work with you! We hope you enjoy their stories!

With gratitude,

Brandelyn N. Anderson

Executive Director
For Love of Children

In memory of Jim and Dani Ritter

Sarah

On May 25, 2020, a Black man named George Floyd was killed by a white policeman.

Even though I'm not Black, I know that racism is wrong. I hate that my friends get harassed for being Black. My best friend Sydney is Black and I get upset that this happens to her. I spent all of June and July protesting with my friends for Black Lives Matter. We were determined to make a change that summer.

One day in June, Sydney and I decided to go to Rock Creek Park. Sydney is my best friend. I've known her since kindergarten. She's my best friend because she is supportive, kind, and doesn't care what others think. She also has the same energy as me so it's really fun being around her.

We stopped every few feet to take pictures of flowers. While we were taking pictures, I overheard a group of kids saying racist things to Sydney. Sydney looked scared and like she was about to cry. When I saw that, I went over and confronted the group.

"Stop it!" I said. "How would you feel if someone said hurtful things to you? Or made fun of you for how you look? You don't even know how much what you're saying hurts people."

The kids walked away from us and I gave Sydney a hug. I had been practicing what to do if I saw someone being bullied. There had been a lot of videos online of racist interactions and I was worried I might see it happen one day. I told the kids to stop and asked them how they would feel if they switched places. They left.

Sydney and I left the park and went to get ice cream. While we were on our way, I kept thinking about what happened and wondered why people are racist. It doesn't make sense to me.

I asked Sydney if she was okay after being harassed at the park. "Thank you for asking. I'm fine but I still feel uncomfortable. They really hurt my feelings." Sydney said.

"I'm so sorry," I told her. "And I can kind of understand how you feel. I've been bullied before. I want you to know I am here to comfort you."

Sydney thanked me and told me that she trusts me. It made me feel good to be able to support my friend. "Thanks for trusting me," I said to Sydney.

Sydney smiled and we worked on protest posters all afternoon.

One day, while out with my family, I saw one of the kids from the group that harassed Sydney. When he spotted me in the crowd, he waved and walked over to me. "Do you remember me?" The kid asked.

"I do," I looked him up and down. He was wearing a t-shirt that had "Black Lives Matter" printed on the front. "My name's Jason. I'm sorry about what happened at the park the other day. My friends were being jerks and they shouldn't have said those things." he said to me. "Why didn't you tell them that?" I asked him, frowning.

"I was afraid of what they would say." Jason must have seen the disappointment in my eyes because he looked away and said, "I didn't really get what was going on. And most of the people I know want to avoid talking about it. I thought you were brave for standing up for your friend and in front of so many people."

Jason told me that after that day in the park, he felt embarrassed by his friends. Jason said that when he started paying attention to the news and realized how big the problem was, he started to understand.

I yanked off my backpack remembering that I had some flyers about our protest that Sydney made. I handed one of the flyers to Jason and told him that he should come. "Thanks. I will tell my parents I want to go," Jason said.

"That sounds good. I think you owe my friend, Sydney, an apology. You can do that when we see you at the protest."

Jason nodded and thanked me again. I walked away with my family and pulled out myphone to call Sydney.

Truth

Spoiled, sassy, and classy! That's me. Truth!

I'm a true California girl. I love the sun, I love shopping, and I love hanging out with my friends. Our friend group is full of energetic, adventurous kids and we always have so much fun together.

Well, we did. But then everything changed. one day, my parents sat down with me and my siblings and gave us some big news. We were moving! And we weren't just moving into a new house, but across the country to Washington, DC. I was nervous and excited at the same time. There were going to be a lot of new things for me to see and explore which was exciting. However, I knew I'd miss my friends so much and that made me nervous.

At first, the move was a struggle for me. But after a while, I started to enjoy myself. There were lots of museums and parks where my family spent a lot of time together. And the food here is amazing!

Although I was having a lot of fun in my new home, there was still something missing. I was having trouble finding a friend group. I was so used to my big group so I felt a little sad and anxious without them.

Then I met Adeline and Shyla.

One day, I was spending some time in Rock Creek Park with my family. We got icees and went for a nature walk. I was stumbling around holding my head with the craziest brain freeze ever! I bumped into someone and when I turned around I saw Adeline.

Adeline was taking nature pictures and collecting rocks. It turns out she also had a brain freeze which made us both laugh. We started talking and found out we had so much in common! We talked and played for an hour that day.

Adeline and I hung out a lot. She introduced me to her friend Shyla and the three of us became an inseparable group. We were all just alike. Anytime we could be, the three of us were together.

When COVID-19 hit, Adeline, Shyla, and I weren't able to see each other as much as we usually did. We kept in touch over Facetime just about every day. It wasn't the same, of course, but we still had a lot of fun together.

At the end of May, a white police officer in Minneapolis murdered a Black man named George Floyd. Protests in support of Black Lives Matter erupted all over the country. Tensions were really high everywhere. That tension made its way into my friend group as well.

On our Facetime calls, I noticed that Shyla was starting to become distant. She didn't talk as much, if she even answered the phone at all. Adeline and I both texted her to see if she was okay, she said that she was fine. After missing four of our scheduled calls, I decided to call Shyla myself and ask her what was going on.

At first Shyla tried to deny that anything was wrong, but after a while she finally told me."I've been avoiding Adeline."

I was shocked, "Did she say something mean to you?"

"No, nothing like that. I've been feeling sad a lot lately." she said.

"Because of the protests and everything?" I asked.

"Yeah," she sighed.

"I know," I nodded. "I get sad out of nowhere sometimes. Even when I'm distracting myself on purpose. I just don't know what's going to happen next."

'Me too!" Shyla exclaimed. "It seems like anything could happen. I'm scared."

Shyla's family are Black Dominican. They all watch the news together every night because Shyla's parents say that Black kids need to stay informed about the world around them. They say that their parents didn't share enough with them and they don't want Shyla to have to go through what they went through.

My family is Black, too. Back in California, we had lots of conversations as a family about racism and police safety. My older brother experienced racial profiling when walking on the street with a hoodie on and my older sister experienced racial profiling while shopping at a grocery store.

Shyla and I talked for two hours about everything. At the end of our conversation, I asked if she would join me and Adeline on Facetime tomorrow.

"Sometimes, it's awkward to be on Facetime with Adeline and she's talking about games or nails or something and I have all this on my mind. She just doesn't get it."

See, Adeline is white. Her parents think she's too young to know about the realities of racism. I get that Adeline's parents don't want her to worry but I also understand that Shyla wants Adeline to be more sensitive. I have to admit, It would be nice if both of my best friends could share all of our feelings. I decided to talk to my mom about what to do.

"I love both of them. They're my best friends...but I get what Shyla's saying. It makes me feel bad too when I have to hold my feelings in, too," I said to my mom.

My mom gave me a hug and told me that it's okay to have a bunch of different feelings. A few nights later she had a video call with Shyla and Adeline's parents about everything. They talked for hours but I was in my room and could not hear anything.

The next day, my mom took me on a mommy-daughter adventure day. We bought new press-on nails, went to see an outdoor art installation, and then ended the day with pizza and milkshakes at Rock Creek Park. I drank my milkshake really fast and got a brain freeze of course!

"Truth, I want to talk to you about my conversation with Shyla and Adeline's parents." My mom turned to me with a warm look on her face.

"Okay," I said.

"As your parents, it's our job to help you through confusing situations like this one. Just like most things in life, you will learn from this experience. But it may be difficult while it is happening. Us parents had an uncomfortable conversation last night, but we pushed through it because we value our friendship and the friendship between you three girls."

"Okay, I understand," I replied. I had been pretty nervous the night before when our parents were talking for so long.

"I also want to tell you that this probably will not be the last time that you and your friends feel awkward about things, especially when it comes to race. Part of being a good friend is learning about and believing in each other, especially when you can't relate. Last night, I told Adeline's parents that she has to know more about the things you and Shyla go through in order to be a good friend. It isn't fair to you and Shyla to have to hide your feelings." My mom grabbed my hand and held it in hers.

She said that Adeline's parents had agreed to start having hard conversations. They didn't want her to lose her friends. Shyla's parents suggested that each family talk separately and come up with suggestions for what to do next. After that, we could all talk together. My mom and I made a list of ideas:

- *When we get on facetime together, we should ask how each other is feeling. That way if one of us is having a bad day, we can talk about that and support that person.*
- *If there's a time that Shyla only wants to talk to me, she could text me.*
- *Whenever any of us doesn't want to talk, we won't pressure each other. That doesn't mean you don't like us anymore.*
- *Whenever we have a question about the hard stuff, we can ask our parents and they have to answer. Our friendship depends on it!*

As we were leaving the park, we saw a flyer for a Black Lives Matter protest just for kids. My mom took a picture of a flyer and sent it to Shyla and Adeline's parents. She told me she was going to ask if we, kids and parents, go together.

Jan

My dad and I ride our bikes together every weekend. It's our favorite thing to do. We always ride bikes in Rock Creek Park. I love being able to go fast and see new places whizzing by in a blur.

One weekend, we took a new path and rode over a bridge made of rocks. At the end of the bridge I saw a sign with red and green letters. When I got closer, I saw that the poster said "BLACK LIVES MATTER" in big letters. I got off my bike to take a closer look.

The poster said that there was going to be a kid's protest here in the park in a few days. I pulled out my phone to check my calendar when I heard my dad's voice over my shoulder.

"Don't even think about it," he says.

I turn around and look up at my dad. His eyes are big.

"Come on, Dad. I really want to go," I pleaded.

"You can't go. You're too young and it's too dangerous. Haven't you seen the news and videos online?"

"But Dad -"

"End of discussion. I make the rules. You can't go."

I tried asking him one more time, but my dad wouldn't change his mind. He said that I should let the adults handle it. I was so frustrated.
I couldn't think of anything else for the rest of the ride. My head started to hurt.

The next day, I talked with my friend, Alexa. I told her that my dad was worried about my safety at the protest. Alexa is older than me and had been to protests before. Alexa said that happened to her too so she and her parents decided to make a safety plan together. I thought that was a great idea! I decided to sit down with my dad and tell him that I understand why he's worried but that I feel strongly about supporting Black people in this fight.

I asked my dad if we could make a safety plan together. I suggested that my dad talk with Alexa's parents about how they stay safe at the protests and I asked my dad to go with me. My dad agreed and said we couId go to the protest together!

At the protest there are a lot of posters. Many of them say "Black Lives Matter." It's exciting to be marching with other people who want justice for the Black members of our community. There are other people from my school there: teachers, janitors, students. My dad and I are in charge of putting up more posters so that other people will see the message. After the protest, my dad took me and my friend Shaggy to get ice cream. While we were sitting outside eating, my dad told me he was proud of me for standing up for what I believe in and supporting my friends and the Black community.

Alexa

The mid-afternoon June sun pours into the open window and reflects off the silver spiked choker and bracelet I'm wearing. I pull my black and purple faux leather jacket over a plain, black crop top, and flip my matching black and purple ombre hair from under the collar. My solid black tights almost blend into the black skirt I have on. I grab my best black eyeliner and very precisely give myself tiny lightning bolts on the sides of each eye. I slip on my favorite black combat boots over my tights and take one last look in the mirror before I leave.

I lift my arms slowly up and over my head and wiggle my fingers as high as I can. Then, I curl my fingers and bend my elbows, mimicking claws ready to attack. I let out a big breath with my mouth wide open and tongue out. "Hhhhhhhhuuuuuuhhhhhhhh"

"You are you and that's more than enough," and with a wink and a finger gun, I'm out the door.

I don't always do a lion's breath before leaving the house, and I definitely don't usually wink at myself {okay, I do), but some days I need a little more encouragement than others.

I am no stranger to feeling othered. I'm a 8th grade girl who likes horror and romance movies, wears a lot of black eyeliner, and acts a little weird. I have always been bullied for my interests, but when I decided to cut my hair two years ago, the bullying got so much worse.

Kids would stare and call me "weirdo," "killer clown," or "serial killer." This hurt a lot. I felt misunderstood and punished for just being myself. I tried everything I could to ignore the bullying but it didn't stop. I became really, really stressed. This went on for two years.

Eventually, I reached my breaking point. I told my parents that I couldn't take it anymore. My parents were upset when I finally told them what had been happening. "Why didn't you say anything the first time it happened?" they asked.

I told my parents that I tried talking to the adults at school but nothing they did helped. We talked for a long time and my parents decided to get me into therapy.

Going to therapy was great. I learned strategies for managing my anxiety and stress. I also learned that it's okay for me to be different from the kids around me.

Sarah and I became friends the first time we met. We were both at the library studying and started talking. Eventually, Sarah introduced me to her friends and we all began meeting at a library to study and play games together. It was a lot of fun hanging out with them because they were super nice and really supportive of each other.

Then one day, they asked me the dreaded question, "Why do you wear all black clothing and black eyeliner all the time?"

I was worried that they were going to make fun of me but I decided to be honest. I responded, "I am really into rock stuff and I've wanted to be goth since I was little."

"Cool!" they all said together.

I told them that I thought they were going to make fun of me because that's what always happens.

"It doesn't matter who or what you are. You are welcome in our friend group," Sarah said.

Everyone else agreed and said that friends are supposed to support each other. I was elated. It had been so hard to find kids my age that accepted me for me. Hearing this from them made me very happy.

Today, I'm going to meet my friends because Sarah told me about the protest she and Sydney are putting together. They asked me to bring art supplies to make posters for the march.

Sarah told me that she and her friends wanted to put together this protest to help other kids learn about the Black Lives Matter movement and racism. She said they were also hoping to get the attention of adults and encourage them to do more to help kids deal with our feelings and teach us about what's going on.

I agreed to help out and bring my art supplies because I know how it feels to be harassed because of how you look. My new friends helped me gain a lot of my confidence back. I want to help other people become as strong as I am now. That's why I want to support my Black friends and other Black people.

Everyone should be free to be themselves.

Darwin

I am an artist. I've been drawing since I was three years old and my favorite thing to draw is animals. I love animals so much and it's fun to show their unique personalities through my art.

One of my teachers helped me enter a mural painting contest. And guess what? Out of over 50 applications, I was one of four students chosen to participate. We get to come up with ideas for the mural as a group and paint it ourselves. I am so excited.

I feel most creative when I'm outdoors so I decided to go out on a walk at Rock Creek Park to look for inspiration. I took pictures of the tall trees and fragrant flowers. After walking around for about an hour, I ran into Shaggy. He was walking toward me with his dog and cat together.

I was shocked because I had NEVER seen a dog and a cat getting along.

I called out to Shaggy and his dog saw me and wagged his tail. I asked how he gets his dog and cat to get along with each other so well. He shared all the training tricks and told me about the other animals he has at home. Shaggy and I talked for a while and we learned that we both love animals. I asked Shaggy if it was okay for me to take a picture of his dog and cat.

He said yes.

After we said goodbye, I kept walking and couldn't stop thinking about Shaggy's dog and cat. How did he do that?

I started to hear a faint noise in the distance. I followed the noise and stumbled upon a Black Lives Matter protest. The group was made up of mostly kids. They were protesting and chanting, "Black Lives Matter". I watched for a while and asked if I could take pictures. They all agreed.

I admired their signs while I took pictures. My favorite poster was green and in big bold letters said, "Black lives should be treated fairly!"

I took a look through my photos while sitting on a bench a few feet away from the protest. I came across the photo I took of Shaggy's dog and cat. I remembered how easily the dog and cat get along even though they are not supposed to. I wonder why people can't do the same thing?

I think people should learn to respect each other no matter what they look like because if cats and dogs can get along so can people. What should I paint for my mural? Maybe I could capture the love that his dog and cat have for each other? I took out my sketchbook and started drawing.

One of the kids from the protest came over to see what I was drawing. She told me she loved the drawing and asked me if I could draw a few more for her friends. I started drawing as many sketches as I could so that they could all have one. I made so many posters that I lost count! It was great to be helpful to the kids that were protesting. After making all those posters, I was pretty tired, so I sat down to watch the rest of the protest. I decided that when the protest was over, I was going to ask some of the kids to have a drawing competition with me!

Shaggy

Ever since I was little, my mom has always said to me, "You're going places. You're a big dreamer." And she's right. I have big dreams.

I want to be an actor and a rapper one day...Most importantly though, I want to be a veterinarian. I love animals. All animals. And I have a lot of pets!

My favorite channel is Animal Planet and my favorite show to watch is The Zoo. I do tons of research and use what I learn from the show to care for my pets. I'm most proud of how well my dog and cat get along with each other.

My dog, Prince, and my cat, Big Gangsta, were both young when they came to my family, so they grew up together and love each other a lot.

One day, while watching my favorite show, I got a news alert on my phone. The alert stated that the police had murdered another unarmed Black person. I muted the tv and felt sad. I kept thinking about how easily that could be me.

I am Black.

I couldn't focus on the show anymore. I decided to take my dog and cat out for a walk to clear my mind. I went to Rock Creek Park because it's huge and there are so many different types of animals that I could possibly see.

We walked for about an hour and then stopped to play. Big Gangsta sat on my shoulders while Prince chased his tail in a circle.

I saw Darwin walking up to me and I could tell he wanted to talk about my dog and cat. He had that look in his eyes. I wasn't really in the mood to talk but Prince started to pull on the leash toward Darwin. The conversation couldn't be avoided.

Darwin and I realized how much we had in common, we both loved animals more than anything else in the world. We talked for a long time. After we said goodbye and parted ways, I felt a little better. I noticed that during my entire conversation with Darwin, another Black boy, I didn't even think about what our skin looked like.

I was happy to have made that connection with Darwin.

Suddenly, Big Gangsta took off after a rabbit he'd spotted. I held on tight to Prince's leash and we chased the cat together. We ran up the dirt path, through bushes and trees, for what seemed like forever. When we finally caught up, Big Gangsta was sitting on the shoulders of Jan, one of my friends. Jan's dad stood next to him laughing.

Jan told me that he and his dad were here for the protest. I looked around and saw some people I knew: Sarah, Alexa, Truth, and Darwin were all there. Sarah was holding a bullhorn and leading the group in chants. Alexa was handing out masks and water. Truth was talking with two of her friends and their parents. Darwin was helping to make posters. I joined in the protest.

Across the field, I noticed Darwin taking pictures and waved. Darwin smiled and waved back. I felt happy to see my friends at the park protesting for Black Lives Matter.

During the protest, some kids got up to give speeches. Sarah spoke first. "Your voice matters and we're all human and should get along. I am here to protest with signs that are the truth because Black Lives Do Matter."

A few more kids spoke and I decided that I wanted to speak to the entire group, too. I'm Black and have a lot to say about my experiences. It's important for people to hear the truth from somebody who lives it every day.

"Black Lives Matter. I am here today because I feel comfortable and because you treat me like family. I want everyone to feel comfortable all the time. I want everyone to feel like a family. Let no one hold you down, and if you can't get up then get going forward. Don't be afraid and ashamed of your skin and your feelings. Let no one tell you what to do because you do what you have to do."

Kurtis: To my family because they're very supportive - even the ones I don't see anymore.

Jan: To all of the people who encouraged me to learn math because when you write a book you need to know the measurements.

Sarah: To my mom for always being there and giving me opportunities she did not have as a little girl.

Aziyah: To my grandma for always being kind, supportive and loving me the way I am.

Valerie: To my mom for always being there and encouraging me to try new things.

Amir: To Chadwick Boseman for being a Black Lives Matter Superhero and giving us something to be proud of.

FLOC: To 826DC for guiding and supporting our students through the writing process. Your guidance and expertise helped them find their voice.

FLOC: To the FLOC staff for continuously creating a safe space for our students to be uniquely themselves!